Pony Pals

He's My Pony!

Jeanne Betancourt

Illustrated by Paul Bachem

A
LITTLE APPLE
PAPERBACK

SCHOLASTIC INC.

New York   Toronto   London   Auckland   Sydney
Mexico City   New Delhi   Hong Kong   Buenos Aires

For Shelly Studenberg

Thank you to Christine Sierau of
Blue Rider Stables for sharing her knowledge
of ponies and riders. Thank you, also,
to Brandy Buckingham.

No part of this publication may be reproduced in whole or in part, or stored in a retrieval system, or transmitted in any form or by any means, electronic, mechanical, photocopying, recording, or otherwise, without written permission of the publisher. For information regarding permission, write to Scholastic Inc., Attention: Permissions Dept., 555 Broadway, New York, NY 10012.

ISBN 0-439-21641-9

Copyright © 2001 by Jeanne Betancourt.
All rights reserved. Published by Scholastic Inc.

SCHOLASTIC, LITTLE APPLE PAPERBACKS, and associated logos are trademarks and/or registered trademarks of Scholastic Inc.

12 11 10 9 8 7 6 5 4 3 2 1   1 2 3 4 5 6/0

Printed in the U.S.A.
First Scholastic printing, September 2001

Contents

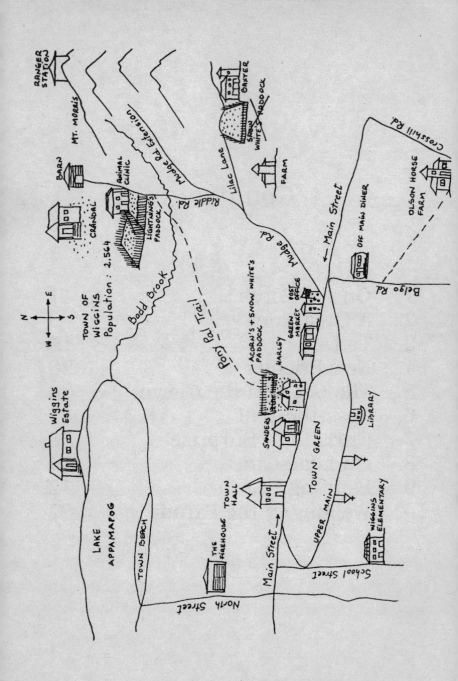

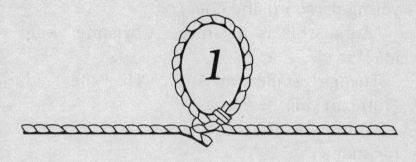

On the Porch

Anna Harley was in the paddock with her Shetland pony, Acorn. She scratched Acorn's thick mane. Acorn whinnied gently. He loved attention.

"Anna, Anna," a voice shouted.

Anna's next-door neighbor, Ms. Pucci, was motioning to Anna. Ms. Pucci wanted Anna to come to her house. Anna left Acorn and ran toward her neighbor's backyard.

Ms. Pucci was on her porch. A girl with straight blond hair stood beside her. The girl was leaning on a walker. Anna had seen old people using walkers. But she'd never seen a young person using one.

"Anna, this is my niece, Christine," said Ms. Pucci.

The girl smiled at Anna. "Hi," she said. "You can call me Chris."

"I'm just Anna," said Anna. "I don't have a nickname."

"Christine is staying with me this week," said Ms. Pucci. "I hope you and your friends will play with her."

Christine rolled her eyes. Anna knew she was embarrassed by what her aunt said. She grinned at Christine. "Glad to meet you," she said.

The phone rang and Ms. Pucci went inside to answer it.

"I've been watching your ponies," said Christine. "They're so beautiful. I love how they run around together."

"The brown-and-black Shetland is mine," explained Anna. "His name is Acorn. The other pony is Snow White. She belongs to

Lulu. Our friend Pam has a chestnut-colored pony named Lightning."

"Acorn, Snow White, and Lightning," said Christine. "Those are nice names. I did some drawings of Acorn and Snow White. Want to see?"

"Sure," said Anna. "I like to draw, too."

Anna followed Christine to a table on the porch. Christine showed her two drawings of the ponies that were done in pencil and felt-

tipped pen. In one, the ponies were grazing side by side. In another, they were running together.

Anna liked the drawings a lot. "You draw ponies great," she told Christine. "And I love the bright colors you use."

"I love ponies," said Christine.

"Me, too," said Anna. She looked at the walker. "Can you ride? I mean, do you ride?"

"No," said Christine. "I was born with cerebral palsy. That's why I need the walker. My whole left side is sort of screwy."

"That's too bad," said Anna.

"It's no big deal," said Christine cheerfully. "It's part of who I am. It's me." She looked toward Anna's house. "Somebody is at your back door."

"That's Lulu," said Anna. She waved for Lulu to come over to Ms. Pucci's.

Anna introduced Lulu and Christine to each other. Lulu loved Christine's drawings. "Anna does great drawings of ponies, too," she told Christine.

"We should draw together sometime,

Anna," said Christine. "Lulu and Pam can model for us. We'll do their portraits. I love to draw faces. That would be so much fun."

"I don't know if I can stay still for very long," said Lulu. "But I could try."

Anna didn't like to draw faces. She didn't think that she was very good at it. She glanced down at Christine's pictures of the ponies. She thought Christine was a much better artist than she was.

Anna looked at her watch. "We're supposed to meet Pam soon," she said. "To go for a trail ride."

"Can the three of you come over after your ride?" asked Christine. "I'd love to meet Pam."

"Sure," said Anna and Lulu together.

"We'll ride for about an hour," said Anna, "then we'll all come back here."

"Great," said Christine.

Anna and Lulu said good-bye and left.

"Christine is nice," said Lulu as they went out to the paddock. "I like her."

"Me, too," said Anna. But she didn't want

to draw and paint with Christine — especially faces.

Anna and Lulu saddled up their ponies and rode onto Pony Pal Trail. Pony Pal Trail was a mile-and-a-half woodland trail that connected the Harley paddock with the Crandals' big field. It was a perfect shortcut for the Pony Pals.

Pam was waiting for Anna and Lulu at the three birch trees. The girls moved their ponies into a circle.

Lulu and Anna told Pam all about Christine. Then the three friends went on their trail ride. They rode slowly at first, so they could talk some more. Lulu said it was too bad that Christine didn't ride.

"She loves ponies," said Anna.

"My mother has a riding student who uses crutches," said Pam, "and another one who uses a walker. Maybe Christine could ride, too."

"Remember that woman who used to own Acorn?" asked Lulu. "She used crutches."

"Sally Southack," remembered Anna. "She

had cerebral palsy, too. Sally rode Acorn for eight years. Now she rides a horse." Anna stopped Acorn and turned in the saddle to face her friends. "Let's help Christine ride. She's so crazy about ponies. She'll love it."

"We'll get my mother to give her lessons," suggested Pam. "We can ride in the ring with her."

"It's a great idea," said Lulu.

I'd rather help Christine ride than draw portraits with her, thought Anna.

The riders came to a straight, smooth section of the trail. Anna patted Acorn's neck. "Let's go, Acorn," she said.

Acorn snorted happily and moved into a smooth gallop. Anna leaned forward. She felt the air blow across her cheeks. She loved to gallop on Acorn.

When the trail came to a sharp turn, Anna slowed Acorn down. Anna thought about Christine again. Would she really be able to ride?

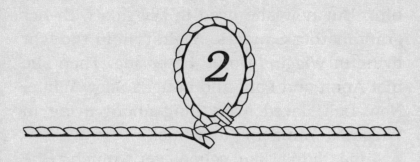

A Great Idea

The Pony Pals rode back to the Harley paddock. While Anna was taking off Acorn's tack, she thought about her two best friends.

Pam Crandal had been her friend since kindergarten. Pam's mother was a riding teacher and her father was a veterinarian. Pam's mother would be a great riding instructor for Christine.

Lulu Sanders' mother died when she was little. Her father studied wild animals. Mr. Sanders traveled all over the world to do his work. For a long time, Lulu traveled with him. But now she lived in Wiggins with her grandmother Sanders. At first, Lulu thought living in Wiggins would be boring. Then she met Anna and Pam and bought Snow White. Now Lulu loved everything about living in Wiggins, even going to school.

Anna didn't like school very much. She was dyslexic, so reading and writing were difficult for her. Sometimes Lulu and Anna did their homework together. Lulu always finished first.

Anna loved to draw and paint. Pam and Lulu told Anna she was a great artist. Anna remembered Christine's drawings of Acorn and Snow White. I'm not as good an artist as Christine, she thought.

While Lulu gave the ponies water, Anna put Acorn's saddle in the shelter. When she came out, Christine was coming toward the paddock.

Pam and Lulu ran over to meet her.

Pam opened the gate for Christine. "I'm Pam," she said.

"Hi," said Christine. "Now I've met all the Pony Pals."

"Come in and meet our ponies," said Lulu.

Christine slowly moved her walker through the gate.

Pam pointed to Lightning. "That's my pony, Lightning," she said.

"Everyone rubs Lightning's white marking for good luck," Lulu told her.

"It's an upside-down heart," observed Christine. "That's so cute."

"I'll bring Lightning over so you can rub it," offered Pam. Pam went to get Lightning.

Anna saw that Christine's left leg was shaking. She wondered if that was because of the cerebral palsy.

Meanwhile, Lulu brought Snow White up to Christine. Christine said Snow White was beautiful.

Acorn trotted over to say hello, too. There were three ponies around Christine now.

"They're all nice ponies," she said.

Anna noticed that Christine's voice was

shaking a little. Is she nervous? wondered Anna. Is she afraid of our ponies?

Pam pulled Lightning's head close to Christine. "Now you can rub the heart," she said.

Can Christine let go of her walker to touch Lightning? wondered Anna. "Chris, you can lean on me," she offered.

"Thanks," said Christine. She put an arm around Anna's shoulder and leaned on her. "Am I too heavy?" she asked.

"No, you're okay," said Anna.

Christine reached out with her right arm and rubbed Lightning's heart. Acorn pushed in between Snow White and Lightning. He wanted to get closer to Christine.

Christine let go of Anna's shoulder and grabbed onto her walker. It's hard for her to stay balanced, thought Anna.

"Let's go have our snack now," suggested Christine. "I made you chocolate chip cookies."

Lulu smacked her lips. "Sounds good to me," she said.

The Pony Pals and Christine went through the gate. Anna closed it behind them. Acorn hung his head over the gate and whinnied as if to say, "Hey, I want to go, too."

The four girls went to the porch. They sat around the table and ate chocolate chip cookies and drank lemonade.

Christine asked a lot of questions about the ponies. The girls told her some of their Pony Pal adventures. Christine loved all their stories.

Ms. Pucci sat on the porch swing and listened.

"Chris, you could take riding lessons at my mother's riding school," said Pam. "If you want."

Christine hesitated. "I guess I could try," she said.

Ms. Pucci stopped swinging. "Christine can't ride," she told the girls.

"Pam's mother is an excellent teacher," said Lulu.

"I'm sure she is," agreed Ms. Pucci. "But I

think riding would be too difficult for Christine." She smiled at her niece. "You understand, dear."

Christine sat up a little taller. She looked her aunt right in the eye. "It's good to try new things," she said. "Even when they're difficult. I want to take riding lessons."

"The woman who used to own Acorn has cerebral palsy," Anna told Ms. Pucci. "She said riding helped her walk better."

"My parents like me to try difficult things, Aunt Helen," said Christine. "I took the bus here all by myself. It was a five-hour trip."

"My mother can call Chris's mother and talk to her about it," added Pam.

"That would be absolutely necessary," said Ms. Pucci. "I can't take the responsibility."

Pam and Christine went inside to call their mothers about the lessons. Anna and Lulu cleared the table while Ms. Pucci watered the plants on the porch.

Pam and Christine finally came back out to the porch. They were both smiling.

"What happened?" asked Anna.

"I talked to my mom," said Christine excitedly. "Pam talked to her mom. Then the two moms talked to each other. My mom called us back." She laughed. "It was a lot of phone calls."

"But it's all settled," announced Pam. "Chris has a riding lesson tomorrow at ten."

"And I'm invited to a barn sleepover at Pam's tomorrow night, Aunt Helen," Christine told Ms. Pucci. "Isn't that the best?"

Ms. Pucci put an arm around Christine and gave her a hug. "It *is* the best," she said.

Christine sat on the porch swing between Pam and Lulu. Anna sat on the porch rail facing them.

"I was afraid I'd be bored here," said Christine. "But I haven't been for a minute. And now I'm going to learn how to ride."

"Wait until you hear about the Fair on the Green, Chris," said Lulu. "It's this Saturday."

"It's on the town green," added Lulu, "which is right in front of our houses."

"What's the fair like?" asked Christine.

"People sell arts and crafts," said Anna. "There'll be a carousel and a Ferris wheel."

"And a lot of yummy food," added Lulu.

"All the profits from the fair go to help Saint Francis Animal Shelter," put in Pam. "They take care of orphaned animals. All kinds of animals. They even have goats. I hope the fair raises a lot of money."

"My mother will have a big food tent," said Anna.

Pam gave the porch swing a little push with her foot. "Anna's mother owns Off-Main Diner," she told Christine. "It's the best diner in town."

"It's the *only* diner in town," giggled Anna.

Christine held up her hands. "Wait!" she exclaimed. "I have an idea."

"What?" said the Pony Pals in unison.

"Let's have a face-painting booth at the fair," she said. "My friends and I did face painting at our school fair last year. We made a lot of money. And everyone had fun at our booth."

"Face painting," said Lulu thoughtfully. "That's a great idea."

"And we have two artists to paint faces," said Pam.

"Anna and I will need your help, too," Christine told Pam and Lulu. "There's lots to do at a face-painting booth. But don't worry. I know how to organize it."

Anna looked out at the ponies. A face-painting booth is a good idea, she thought. I wish I'd had that idea. But I don't think I want to paint faces with Christine.

"Let's have a meeting about the booth tomorrow," suggested Pam. "After your riding lesson, Chris."

"Meanwhile, Anna and I will be thinking of ideas for faces," said Christine. "Okay, Anna?"

Anna turned back to the girls on the porch. "Okay," she agreed. "It'll be fun." She smiled at Christine and her friends. She hoped that face painting with Christine would be fun. But she wasn't sure it would be.

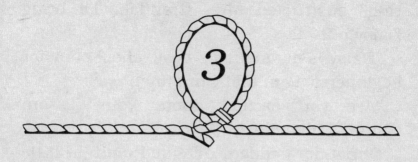

To Do

The next morning, Anna and Lulu rode their ponies over to Pam's. Pam met them at the paddock and helped them unsaddle their ponies.

"Is Christine here yet?" asked Lulu.

"She's in the barn with my mother," answered Pam.

A few minutes later, Christine and Mrs. Crandal came over to the paddock.

"I brought a sleeping bag and a lot of art supplies," Christine told the Pony Pals. "I put them in the barn office."

"You girls go with Christine to the riding ring," instructed Mrs. Crandal. "I'll bring Daisy out."

"Daisy is my mother's best school pony for beginners," Pam told Christine.

"Are you excited about your lesson, Chris?" Lulu asked.

Christine nodded. "Excited and a little nervous, too," she said.

The Pony Pals and Christine went to the riding ring. A ramp with a platform was set up at the side of the ring.

Mrs. Crandal led Daisy to the ramp. "Come over," she called to Christine.

"Daisy's a pretty blond color," said Christine. "It's the same color as your hair, Anna."

"When a pony or horse is blond, it's called a palomino," explained Pam.

"A Pony Pal *palo*mino," joked Anna.

Christine laughed, but Anna noticed her leg was shaking again.

"Daisy is a very sweet pony, Chris," Anna told her. "You're going to love her."

Christine stopped in front of Daisy. As

Christine reached up to pat Daisy's muzzle, her walker fell over. Daisy snorted in Christine's face and backed up with a start.

Christine screamed. Anna reached out to catch her, but it was too late. Christine fell backward and hit the ground with a thud.

Pam grabbed Daisy and moved her away. Mrs. Crandal and Anna knelt beside Christine.

"She's going to step on me!" cried Christine fearfully.

"Pam has her," Anna told Christine.

"Do you want me to call nine-one-one?" Lulu asked Mrs. Crandal.

"I'm okay," Christine told them. "I fall a lot. I'm used to it."

"Don't get up yet, Christine," Mrs. Crandal said. "Catch your breath."

Christine sat up on her elbow. "I can't get up by myself, anyway," she said.

"When the walker fell, it spooked Daisy," Mrs. Crandal explained. "I'm sorry. The sudden movement frightened her."

"Are you sure your leg's okay?" asked Anna.

Christine's left leg was stiff and shaking. "That's just the way it is all the time," said Christine. She looked around. "I need my walker."

Lulu picked up the walker and put it in front of Christine. Mrs. Crandal and Anna helped her up. Christine's left leg was shaking more than ever. Anna noticed that her left arm was shaking, too.

Mrs. Crandal put an arm around Christine's shoulder. "Are you sure you're not hurt?" she asked.

Christine nodded. "But I don't want to have a lesson today," she said.

She turned her walker around and headed out of the ring. The Pony Pals went with her.

Acorn trotted over to the paddock fence. He hung his head over and whinnied as if to say, "Is she okay?"

Christine didn't even look up at Acorn. She was concentrating hard on walking.

Anna went over to Acorn and patted his

face. "Everything is all right," she told her pony.

Lulu and Pam walked on either side of Christine. Anna ran to catch up with them.

"Let's have our meeting about the face-painting booth now," suggested Lulu.

"We can have it on the big rock in the field," put in Pam.

Christine stopped and looked around at the Pony Pals. "Yes, let's have the meeting," she said.

Anna wondered what they'd talk about at the meeting. She hoped she wouldn't have to do any drawings.

"We'll need to take notes," said Christine.

Pam patted her jacket pocket. "I have my pad and a pen," she said.

The four girls went over to the flat rock and sat down.

"Chris, you should be in charge of the meeting," said Lulu. "Because you've had the most experience."

"Okay," agreed Christine. "The first thing we have to do is make a TO DO list." Christine looked around. "Pam, will you write it?"

Pam pulled out her little pad. "I'm ready," she said.

"We'll need a poster," Christine began, "to advertise our booth."

"Good idea," said Anna.

"We'll put posters up all over town," added Lulu. "Then people will look for our booth at the fair."

"And our booth should have a sign," suggested Pam. "So people can find us easily."

"That's important," agreed Christine.

"I have an idea," said Lulu. "Let's take instant photos of our clients."

"That way, they'll have a souvenir," agreed Christine.

"And we'll make more money for the animal shelter," added Lulu.

Anna tried to think of an idea for the booth, but her mind was a blank.

But Lulu, Pam, and Christine kept coming up with ideas. The three girls discussed them. Pam took notes.

Finally, the TO DO list was complete.

TO DO BEFORE THE FAIR

Make:
1. posters to advertise
2. sign for the booth

Borrow from Lulu's grandmother:
1. 4 folding chairs
2. 2 plastic bibs from beauty parlor
3. 2 hand mirrors

Buy:
1. 2 sets of face paints
2. film for instant camera
3. 2 boxes of tissues

Find:
1. box for collecting money and making change
2. 2 small tables for paints and brushes

Anna and Chris will make five face designs each.

TO DO AT THE FAIR
1. Pam collects money and keeps customers in line.
2. Anna and Chris paint faces.
3. Lulu takes photos.

"I already have some ideas for face designs," said Christine.

"Tell us," said Lulu. "Pam can write them down, too."

"I'm going to draw my ideas," said Christine. She grinned around at her new friends. "But I don't want to tell you what they are going to be."

Anna leaned forward. "Why not?" she asked.

"It'll be a quiz," explained Christine. "I'll see if you can guess what they are. That way I'll know if they're good."

"That'll be fun," said Lulu. She turned to Anna. "We'll guess what your five ideas are, too. Okay?"

"Okay," agreed Anna. But she didn't want to do it. What if no one guesses what my face designs are? she wondered. What if Chris does better faces than me? What if all the people at the fair want Chris to paint their faces? What if no one wants me?

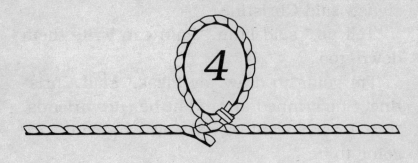

New Friends

Christine pulled herself up on her walker. "That was a great meeting," she said.

Acorn stood at the paddock fence and neighed. Anna looked over at her pony. She knew he wasn't neighing at her.

"What does Acorn want?" asked Christine.

"He's been watching you, Chris," answered Anna. "He's trying to get your attention."

Pam stood up to see Acorn better. "I think Anna's right," she said. "Walk a little bit, Chris. See what happens."

Christine pulled herself up on her walker.

She took a few jerky steps forward. Acorn moved in the same direction. When Christine stopped, he stopped.

"Do it again, Chris," said Lulu.

Christine moved a few more steps. So did Acorn.

"Why is he following me?" asked Christine.

"He's playing with you," said Lulu.

Christine went back to the Pony Pals. Acorn went in the same direction.

"I think he likes your walker," Anna told Christine.

"Daisy didn't like it," Christine said.

"She was spooked when the walker fell over," explained Pam. "Something like that never would have bothered Acorn."

"Acorn loves action," said Lulu. "He was in the circus."

"And in a movie," added Anna. "Nothing spooks him."

Christine sat back down on the rock. "He's really cute," she said.

"We'll prove that Acorn is spook-free," said Anna. "Can I borrow your walker?"

"Sure," said Christine.

Anna carried the walker over to the paddock fence. Lulu took out her whistle and went up to Acorn, too.

Anna shook the walker in front of Acorn's face. He stared at it, but he didn't back away.

"See," Anna called to Christine. "He's not afraid. He's interested in it. He's a very curious pony."

"And he doesn't mind loud noises," added Pam.

Lulu blew her Pony Pal whistle as loud as she could. Acorn's ears went forward, but he stayed calm.

"That's amazing," exclaimed Christine. "Nothing bothers him."

Anna brought the walker back to Christine.

"Acorn can do tricks, too," said Lulu.

"Will he do a trick for me?" asked Christine.

"If I give him the signal, he will," Anna said.

Anna went back to the paddock gate and led Acorn out.

"Have Acorn bow to her," Lulu whispered to Anna.

"That's what I'm going to do," Anna whispered back.

But Anna didn't have time to give Acorn the signal. He turned toward Christine, put one leg forward, and bowed on his own.

He never bows to me without a signal, thought Anna.

Christine pulled herself up on her walker and bent at the waist to bow back. "Hello, Acorn," she said. "Pleased to meet you."

"She's not afraid of Acorn," Lulu told Anna.

Pam came over to Anna and Lulu. "Christine should take riding lessons on Acorn," she said.

"That's what I was just thinking," said Lulu.

Anna was watching Christine and Acorn. Christine was talking to Acorn. All of her at-

tention was on him. And all of *his* attention was on *her.*

"Is that okay with you, Anna?" asked Pam. "Can Christine ride Acorn?"

"Yeah," agreed Anna. "I guess."

Pam and Lulu went over to Christine and Acorn. Anna followed.

"Chris, we have an idea," said Pam.

"We think you should take your riding lessons on Acorn," said Lulu.

Christine looked at Anna. "Could I?" she asked. "You don't mind? Acorn is your pony."

"It's okay," said Anna. "Acorn really likes you. And he won't spook."

Christine sat back down on the rock. "What if my legs don't fit over his back?" she said. "My legs don't spread very far apart."

"You'll ride bareback," Pam told her. "You don't have to fit over a saddle."

Christine still looked worried. "How am I going to stay on Acorn?" she asked. "I can't even stand without a walker."

"My mother will put a special girth on Acorn," explained Pam. "It has handles."

33

"You can do it, Chris," said Lulu. "We'll all be there to help you."

Christine looked up into Acorn's face. "Do you think I can do it?" she asked. Acorn lowered his head onto her lap.

"Look what Acorn's doing!" exclaimed Lulu. "That's so cute."

"Is it a new trick?" Pam asked Anna. "Did you give him a signal?"

"It's not a trick," answered Anna. "He just did it."

Christine stroked Acorn's cheek. "You're a wonderful pony," she said. "You are *very* wonderful."

Acorn never puts his head in my lap, thought Anna. "Okay, Acorn," she said. "Time to go back in the paddock."

"Can't he stay a little longer?" asked Christine.

"We have to find Pam's mother," explained Anna.

"We can talk to my mom later," said Pam.

"Your mother teaches a lot of lessons," insisted Anna. "We have to schedule Chris's lesson now."

"Good point," agreed Lulu.

Anna led Acorn back to the paddock.

"Bye, Acorn," Christine called after him. "See you later."

The four girls headed back to the barn. "You probably won't have a lesson until to-morrow," Pam told Christine. "My mother has a lot of riding lessons today."

Christine looked around at the Pony Pals. "You can go for a trail ride today," she said. "I'll stay here and work on my ideas for face painting."

"Are you sure?" asked Lulu.

"Anna, when you get back you can borrow my art supplies," said Christine.

"That's all right," Anna told her. "I have my own art supplies."

Mrs. Crandal was in the riding ring with a student. "You wait here," Pam told the others. "I'll ask my mother about the lesson."

Pam's six-year-old brother and sister, Jack and Jill, came out of the barn. They ran over to Lulu, Anna, and Christine. Lulu introduced them to Christine.

"Do you always have to walk with that thing?" Jack asked her.

"Yes," answered Christine. "I used to have a wheelchair. I like the walker better."

"I'd like a wheelchair better," said Jack. "You can go faster."

"That's true," said Christine. "In some situations."

Jill ran her hand over the shiny metal of the walker. She smiled up at Christine. "It's pretty," she said.

"Thanks," said Christine.

"Are you taking a riding lesson?" asked Jack.

"I hope so," said Christine. "On Acorn."

"Acorn's the best," said Jack.

"Everybody loves Acorn," Jill told Christine. "My friend Rosalie loves him best, too. She likes to ride him."

"Who's Rosalie?" Christine asked Anna.

"A friend of Jill's who loves ponies," answered Anna.

"Her brother, Mike, bugs us sometimes," added Lulu. "He's older than us. But Rosalie is okay."

"Actually, Mike's okay, too, if he's not with Tommy Rand," Anna told Christine. "Tommy is the real troublemaker."

"Rosalie is coming over to play with me today," Jill said.

"I'd love to meet her," said Christine. "I'll be in the barn office working on face-painting ideas."

"Face painting!" exclaimed Jill.

"Will you paint my face?" asked Jack.

"At the fair on Saturday," Anna told Jill. "We're going to have a booth."

Pam came out of the riding ring. "It's all set," she told Christine. "Nine o'clock tomorrow morning. My mom agreed that Acorn is the perfect pony for you."

Anna looked around. Everyone looked happy. But Anna didn't feel happy.

Acorn is the perfect pony for *me*, she thought. Not Christine. I don't want Christine to ride him. I don't want to share my pony.

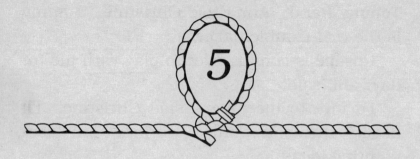

The Cat and the Clown

After lunch, the Pony Pals saddled up their ponies. Christine watched.

"Will you be okay here alone, Chris?" Pam asked.

"I won't be alone," said Christine. "Jack and Jill and their friend Rosalie will be here."

"And Pam's mother and her students," added Lulu.

"And lots of animals," laughed Christine. "I love it here!"

The Pony Pals mounted their ponies, said good-bye to Christine, and rode across the

Crandals' field. Anna led the way onto Pony Pal Trail. Lulu and Pam rode side by side behind her. Anna could hear them talking.

"Chris is great," said Lulu. "She's loads of fun."

"I can't wait to see her face-painting ideas," said Pam.

"It's great that we have *two* artists painting at the booth," said Lulu. "We'll make twice as much money for the animal shelter."

I better think of ideas for face painting, thought Anna. She pictured a cat face. Next she imagined a clown face. But she didn't know how she would paint them.

"Can we go a little faster?" Lulu called to Anna.

Anna realized she'd kept Acorn at a slow walk while she was thinking.

"Sorry," she called back to Lulu. She moved Acorn into a trot.

The Pony Pals rode to their favorite spot on Badd Brook. The ponies drank from the brook and rested. The girls sat on rocks at the edge of the brook and skipped stones.

"It's going to be fun to teach Christine how to ride," said Pam.

"It'll be great to watch her progress," added Lulu.

"Maybe she won't make any progress," said Anna. "What if she can't ride at all?"

"She'll be able to ride," said Pam. "She'll be on Acorn, and we'll be there to help my mother."

Lulu put her hand on Anna's arm. "Don't you like Chris?" she asked.

Anna shook off Lulu's hand. "Of course I like her," she protested. "Everybody likes Chris. She's really nice."

Anna tried to skip a stone. It bounced once and sank to the bottom of the brook. "I thought we'd be trail riding a lot this week," she said. "Just the Pony Pals."

"That's what we're doing now," said Pam.

"I know," said Anna.

Anna also knew that she was being cranky. But she couldn't help it. She went over to Acorn and leaned on his side. Acorn turned and nuzzled her hair. Anna wished she could tell Pam and Lulu the truth. That she didn't like sharing Acorn. And that she didn't want to paint faces with Christine. Tears filled her eyes. She turned away so Lulu and Pam wouldn't see.

"Let's ride back," Pam called to Anna. "We've already been gone over an hour."

Soon the Pony Pals were back on Pony Pal Trail. Pam went first, Lulu followed, and Anna took up the rear. She kept Acorn at a walk. She wanted to be alone with her pony. Suddenly, Acorn stopped and looked around. Anna looked, too.

Mike Lacey was riding toward them on his mountain bike. He pulled up beside them.

"Hi," he said.

"What are you doing here?" asked Anna.

"I was trying to catch up with you," he said. "And I did. I could have beaten you."

"I wasn't racing you, Mike Lacey," said Anna. "I didn't even know you were there." She looked around. "Where's Tommy?"

"He's shooting baskets," answered Mike.

"I'm picking up my sister at the Crandals'. This trail's a great shortcut."

Anna didn't like that Mike used Pony Pal Trail for a shortcut. But at least Tommy Rand wasn't with him.

Pam and Lulu were way ahead of Anna now. Lulu turned to see where Anna was. Anna waved for her and Pam to go on ahead.

Snow White and Lightning don't like bikes riding near them, thought Anna. But Acorn doesn't mind.

Anna gave Acorn the signal to go forward. Mike rode behind them. When they reached the end of the trail, Pam and Lulu were waiting for them.

Rosalie ran across the field to meet Mike and the Pony Pals. Her face was painted.

"Chris painted my face," she shouted excitedly. "Guess what I am. Guess!"

"That's easy," said Mike. "A cat."

"Right!" Rosalie exclaimed as she reached them. "I *am* a cat. Everyone can tell!"

"It's beautiful," exclaimed Lulu. "Chris did a great job."

"You look really cute, Rosalie," said Anna.

Anna thought Christine's face painting of a cat was beautiful, too.

Rosalie stood in front of Acorn. "Can you tell I'm a cat, Acorn?"

Acorn nodded at Rosalie, as if to say yes.

Rosalie kissed him. "I love you, Acorn," she said.

"Let's put our ponies in the paddock," suggested Anna.

"Okay," agreed Pam.

The small group of kids and ponies walked toward the paddock.

"Chris is making Jack into a clown," Rosalie reported. "It's going to be great."

Anna took off her helmet. Christine has already done my only two ideas, she thought. She did both the cat face and clown face.

Rosalie pulled on Anna's arm. "Can I ride Acorn?" she asked. "Please. He has on his saddle and everything."

"Not today," answered Anna. "I'm putting him in the paddock with Snow White and Lightning."

"Just for a little while," begged Rosalie. She patted Acorn's neck. He turned and nuzzled her chest. "See, he wants to give me a ride," she said. "He likes cats."

"Okay," agreed Anna. She handed Rosalie the reins and put the helmet on her. Rosalie put her foot in the stirrup and swung up on Acorn. Anna adjusted the stirrups.

"I'll let her go around the field once," Anna told Pam and Lulu.

"We'll cool down our ponies," said Lulu. She and Pam continued toward the paddock.

"Now stay on the path," Anna instructed Rosalie. "And don't let Acorn eat grass."

Anna walked around the big field with Rosalie and Acorn. Why do I have to share Acorn with *everyone*? she thought. She kicked the grass. Sometimes, it didn't feel like Acorn was her pony.

After Rosalie's ride, Rosalie and Anna put Acorn in the paddock. Rosalie gave him a final hug. "Thanks, Acorn," she said. "Thanks for a great ride."

Anna and Rosalie went to the barn office.

Pam, Lulu, and Mike were watching Christine paint Jill's face. "Just a few more strokes," she told Jill. "And you'll be done, too."

Anna could already tell that Jill was a flower.

"Your faces are great, Chris," said Anna. "But I thought you were going to do them on paper first."

"I had real kids to paint," said Christine. "It was a perfect way to practice."

"I didn't know you had face paints with you," said Anna.

"My aunt bought them for me," said Christine. "She brought them here after you left for the trail ride." She pointed her brush at a bag on the ground. "She bought you a set, too. And brushes and sponges."

Lulu picked up the bag and held it out for Anna. "The jars of paint are big," she said. "So you can do lots of faces."

Anna took the bag from Lulu. I don't want to paint faces with Christine, she thought. I'm not good enough.

Toss-the-Ball

That night, the four girls lay side by side in their sleeping bags on the barn office floor. Christine told them all about her friends at home. She also told them about an operation she had. "My whole body was in a cast for three months," she said.

"That's *awful*," exclaimed Lulu.

"It wasn't as bad as it sounds," said Christine. "Other kids in the hospital had the same thing. We made jokes about it."

Christine is very brave, thought Anna. If I had cerebral palsy, I'd be complaining all the time.

Christine asked the Pony Pals more about their adventures. Anna told her about when Rosalie was lost in the woods. "Acorn is the one who found her," concluded Anna.

"Acorn is a special pony," said Christine.

Finally, everyone stopped talking. Anna waited for them to fall asleep. Then she quietly got up, picked up her bag of face paint supplies, and left the room on tiptoe.

When Anna reached the bathroom, she turned on the light and closed the door. I'll make myself a lion, she decided. Chris didn't do that one. She put jars of yellow and black paint on the back of the sink and looked into the mirror.

First, Anna painted yellow all over her face with a sponge. While it dried, she opened the black paint. She painted black around her eyes, on her nose, and under her nose.

Anna stared at herself in the mirror. I don't look anything like a lion, she thought. I don't even remember what a lion looks like. Does a lion have spots on its face? Do the whiskers show?

Tears gathered in Anna's eyes. I'll never paint faces as well as Christine, she thought.

Black tears ran down Anna's yellow-painted cheeks.

She closed up the paints, washed her face with soap and water, wiped it dry, and went back to her sleeping bag in the barn office. She couldn't sleep. She was more worried than ever about painting faces.

The next morning, after breakfast, Pam and Lulu saddled up their ponies. Anna brushed Acorn and put on his halter. The girls and their ponies went to the riding ring.

Mrs. Crandal and Christine were waiting for them. Christine patted Acorn's head and kissed his cheek. "Hello, Acorn," she said. "I'm going to ride you."

Lulu and Pam mounted their ponies. Anna stayed on the ground with Mrs. Crandal.

Christine walked up the ramp with her walker. Mrs. Crandal helped her mount Acorn, who stood perfectly still the whole time.

Christine looked scared when she finally sat on Acorn. She grabbed the special handles. Her legs looked stiff.

"Don't worry," Mrs. Crandal told Christine. "Acorn won't move until you're ready."

Christine sat taller and looked around. Pam gave her the thumbs-up sign.

"I'm ready," she said.

Anna led Acorn slowly around the ring. Mrs. Crandal walked beside Christine. She adjusted Christine's legs and told her how to balance better.

"Does it hurt anywhere, Christine?" Mrs. Crandal asked.

"I'm all right," answered Christine.

The three riders and ponies went around the ring twice. Mrs. Crandal had them stop. She told Anna to let go of Acorn's lead rope.

"Okay," Mrs. Crandal told Christine. "Acorn won't move until you tell him to."

"How do I tell him?" asked Christine.

"Sit tall, make a clicking sound, and say, 'Move on,' " instructed Mrs. Crandal.

Christine shifted her weight and sat taller

on Acorn. Then she made the clicking sound and said, "Move on."

Acorn moved forward in slow, even steps.

Anna walked beside Acorn and his new rider.

Next, Mrs. Crandal taught Christine how to halt Acorn. When Christine relaxed her seat and said, "Whoa," Acorn stopped.

Anna was proud of her pony.

Pam and Lulu rode their ponies around the ring with Christine. They all started and stopped when Christine told Acorn to.

"Okay, girls," Mrs. Crandal called out. "Let's play ball!" She tossed a medium-size orange ball to Anna.

"Keep your ponies walking," instructed Mrs. Crandal. "Anna will throw you the ball. Try to catch it and throw it back to her."

"I have to let go of the handles to catch it," Christine said nervously. "I'll fall off."

"No you won't," Mrs. Crandal told her. "You can do it."

"I won't throw it to you first, Chris," said Anna.

Anna threw the ball to Pam. Pam threw it back to her. Next, Anna threw the ball to Lulu. When Lulu threw the ball to Anna she threw it to Pam again.

"Throw it to me," said Christine.

Anna turned and carefully threw the ball to Christine. Christine let go of the handles, put out her arms, and caught the ball.

Christine smiled as she threw the ball back to Anna. Anna smiled back. She was happy for Christine.

Ms. Pucci came over to the riding ring, too.

"I'm riding, Aunt Helen," Christine called. "I'm really riding."

"Bravo!" said her aunt.

When the lesson was over, Mrs. Crandal helped Christine dismount. Anna put the walker in front of her.

Acorn didn't move until Christine's weight was on her walker. Then he turned his head to her.

"Thank you, Acorn," Christine said. "Thank you for a wonderful lesson." Acorn lowered his head. She kissed his forehead.

"You did great, Christine," said Mrs. Crandal. "How would you like another lesson tomorrow morning?"

"Can I?" asked Christine excitedly.

"You can have a lesson every day while you're here," Mrs. Crandal told her. "If your aunt doesn't mind."

"I think it's wonderful," said Ms. Pucci. "I'll be happy to be her chauffeur."

Christine looked over at Anna. "Is it okay? I mean, Acorn's your pony."

"I'm always over here, anyway," said Anna. "Besides, Acorn likes you."

"We'll help with the lessons," said Pam.

"It was fun," added Lulu.

They all walked out of the riding ring.

"What are you girls doing with the rest of your day?" asked Mrs. Crandal.

"Christine is coming with me," said Ms. Pucci. "We're visiting her grandmother. But we'll be back this afternoon."

"Let's all go to the diner at four," suggested Lulu. "We'll have another meeting about our face-painting booth."

Anna didn't want to talk about face painting anymore.

"Will I be back by then?" Christine asked her aunt.

"I'll drop you off at the diner," she promised.

"We always have Pony Pal meetings at Anna's mother's diner," Lulu told Christine. "And we eat there, too."

"That'll be so much fun," said Christine. "I'll work on an idea for the poster at my grandmother's."

"Super," said Lulu.

But *I* always make the posters for Pony Pals projects, thought Anna.

"Will you show us your face-painting ideas at the meeting, Anna?" asked Christine.

"Maybe," answered Anna. "I'm still working on them."

"I can't wait to see them," said Christine.

"Anna's a terrific artist," said Pam. "Her ideas will be great."

No, they won't, thought Anna. I don't even have any ideas.

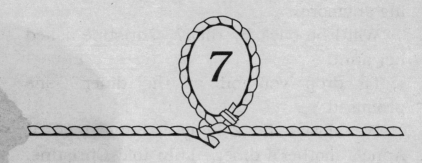

7

Christine's Surprise

After Christine left, Anna and Lulu rode home on Pony Pal Trail.

"Want to come to my house?" Lulu asked Anna.

"No, thanks," answered Anna. "I have to work on my ideas."

Anna went into her house and up to her room. She sat at her desk and opened her sketch pad.

First, she drew a butterfly face. She didn't like it.

Next, she tried a lion face. Then a flower and a clown face.

She didn't like any of them.

She pulled the pages out of her sketch-book and tore them into little pieces. After that, Anna went downstairs and watched television.

At three-thirty, Anna and Lulu met in the paddock. They saddled up their ponies and rode to the diner. Lightning was already tied to the hitching post when they got there.

Anna and Lulu tied their ponies next to Lightning and went inside. Christine and Pam were waiting for them in the Pony Pals' favorite booth.

As she followed Lulu to the booth, Anna thought, I wish Christine wasn't here. I wish we were just the Pony Pals.

A few minutes later, the four girls were sharing a plate of brownies and drinking milk.

"I can't believe I rode Acorn!" exclaimed Christine. "My favorite pony and I rode him. I loved it." She smiled around at the Pony Pals. "Thank you for helping with my lesson."

"It was fun," said Lulu. She took a bite of her brownie.

"Tomorrow we can play a game riding around cones," said Pam. "It'll be good for your balance, Chris."

"How does the game work?" asked Christine.

"We'll all be on our ponies," answered Pam. "Anna will move the cones and — "

"So, what about the face-painting booth?" asked Anna. She had interrupted Pam, but she didn't care.

"What do you mean?" asked Lulu.

"The face-painting booth," repeated Anna. "Aren't we here to have a meeting about that?"

"Of course we are," said Pam. "Do you have your face designs, Anna?"

"That's not what I meant," answered Anna. "I meant, what about the list and everything. The TO DO list."

Pam made a face at Anna. Pam's mad at me for being a grump, thought Anna. Anna

looked down at her napkin and ripped it in half.

"Okay," said Christine. "I have the TO DO list." She took out the list and a pencil.

"I found an old tin box," Pam reported. "It'll be perfect for collecting money."

Christine put a check mark next to "box for collecting money and making change."

"And I asked my grandmother to lend us chairs, bibs, and mirrors," reported Lulu. "She's closing her beauty parlor for the fair. We can borrow whatever we want."

"I found two folding tables in our attic," said Pam. She looked from Christine to Anna. "They'll be perfect for your paints and brushes."

"And I have an idea for the poster," reported Christine. She put a manila folder on the table and opened it. Anna looked down at her torn napkin.

"It's a terrific poster!" exclaimed Pam.

"It's really good," added Lulu. "I love the faces."

Anna finally looked at the poster, too.

Face
Painting

AT WIGGINS FAIR

Choose
from 10
great
designs!

Two
Artists —
NO LONG LINES!

SAT. JUNE 1ST 9a.m.-3p.m.

$2 For Face Painting
& Photo

Chris's poster looks terrific, thought Anna. I could never make a poster that good.

"Why are some of the faces blank?" asked Pam.

"Those are for Anna's face designs," answered Christine. She pushed the poster toward Anna. "After you put in your faces, my aunt will make copies for us."

"Anna, do your faces tonight," said Lulu. "Then we can put the posters up tomorrow."

61

"We'll put them up all over town," Pam told Christine.

"They'll be up for three days before the fair," added Lulu. "A lot of people will see them."

"I have an idea for the sign for our booth, too," said Christine.

"What?" asked Lulu and Pam in unison.

"Anna and I can make life-size drawings of our face designs," she answered. "We can cut them out and paste them to the sign."

"That would look so good," commented Lulu.

"The sign should say the price, too," said Pam.

"And that we're doing photos," added Lulu as she reached for another brownie.

Christine wrote down their ideas for the sign.

Lulu turned to Anna. "What do you think, Anna?" she asked.

"What do I think about what?" asked Anna.

"About our face-painting booth," answered Lulu impatiently. "You haven't said anything at this meeting."

Anna pushed the poster across the table to Christine and stood up. "I think Christine should do all the faces on the poster," she said. "And she should do all the faces at the fair."

"But," said Christine. "I don't want — "

"I have to go," said Anna, interrupting her. She ran out of the diner.

On Lilac Lane

Anna untied Acorn, put on her helmet, and swung into the saddle.

Snow White whinnied as if to say, "Hey, Acorn, where are you going?"

Anna thought Pam and Lulu would come after her. But no one came out of the diner. No one called her name.

She rode down Belgo Road to Main Street and made a left. But she didn't go home. Pam and Lulu still might try to follow me, she thought.

Anna turned onto Mudge Road. I'll go to Lilac Lane, she decided. They won't look for me there.

Anna rode along Mudge Road until she came to Lilac Lane. Lilac Lane was a quiet dirt road. Farmhouses, barns, and cows spread across green fields.

But Anna didn't feel peaceful. She felt angry and upset. Angry, upset tears streamed down her face.

"Hey, wait up," a voice shouted from behind her. It wasn't Pam's or Lulu's voice. It was a boy's voice.

Mike Lacey rode his bike up beside Anna.

"What are you doing?" he asked. "Where's Pam and Lulu?"

Anna halted Acorn. "Stop following me!" she shouted.

"I wasn't following you," he said. "I just saw you." He stared at her. "Hey, what's wrong? Where are Pam and — "

Anna didn't hear the end of the sentence. She moved Acorn into a gallop. When she slowed her pony down, she took a quick peek over her shoulder. Mike wasn't following her anymore.

Why am I so angry? wondered Anna.

I'm angry with Mike because he saw me cry.

I'm angry with Christine for being a good artist.

I'm angry with Pam and Lulu for liking Christine.

I'm angry with Acorn for liking Christine.

But mostly I'm angry with myself, thought Anna. I don't want to share my pony. I don't want anyone to be a better artist than me. I'm selfish.

I hate selfish people.

I hate myself.

Tears filled Anna's eyes again and ran down her cheeks. I'm being mean to everybody, she thought. My friends must hate me, too.

When Anna reached the end of Lilac Lane, she turned Acorn around. Two riders were coming down the road. Lulu and Pam had found her.

"Whoa," Anna told Acorn. He stopped and neighed at Lightning and Snow White. He was glad to see them. I'm not glad to see Pam and Lulu, thought Anna. I'm ashamed of myself.

Lulu and Pam rode up to her.

"Anna, are you okay?" asked Lulu.

Anna shook her head no. "How did you find me?" she asked.

"Mike told us where you were riding," answered Pam.

"He's bugging me," said Anna grumpily. "Everybody's bugging me. Why did you even bother to look for me?"

"Because we're best friends," said Lulu.

"Because we're Pony Pals," added Pam.

Lulu dismounted. "Come on, Anna. Get off Acorn."

"We're having an emergency Pony Pal meeting," explained Pam as she slid off Lightning. "Right now."

Anna slid off Acorn.

The Pony Pals led their ponies to the edge of a field. They tied them to a fence and sat in the grass.

"Where's Christine?" asked Anna. "Did you leave her all by herself?"

"Her aunt picked her up," said Lulu.

"Mike saw me crying," Anna told them. "He better not tell Tommy." Anna looked at her two best friends. "I'm sorry I ran out of the meeting."

"You must have been really upset to do that," said Pam.

Lulu put her arm around Anna's shoulder. "What's wrong?" she asked. "Why did you leave?"

Anna broke off a piece of long grass. "Acorn likes Chris better than me," she said. She tied the grass in a knot.

"No, he doesn't," said Lulu. "Acorn is friendly. That's the kind of pony he is."

"Christine probably reminds Acorn of his first owner," added Pam. "Because of the walker."

Anna made another knot in the grass. Then she looked up at her friends. "Sometimes it's hard to share him," she said.

"Maybe Christine can ride Daisy now," suggested Pam.

Anna shook her head. "It's okay," she said. "Acorn is the best pony for Chris."

"You still look sad," commented Lulu.

"I'm a lousy artist," Anna mumbled. "I don't have any ideas for face painting. Christine's faces are *so* good."

"She got her ideas from a book!" said Pam. "She copied them."

"She copied them!" exclaimed Anna. "I didn't know that. I thought they were all her ideas."

"We all did," said Lulu.

"She was going to show us the book at the meeting," added Pam. "She even had it with her."

The Pony Pals talked for a long time about Christine and Acorn and the face-painting booth.

Suddenly, Anna stood up. "I have to go,"

she said. "I want to tell Christine I'm sorry."

Pam and Lulu stood up, too.

Anna grinned at her two best friends. "And I want to borrow that face-painting book."

The three girls mounted their ponies and rode back to Mudge Road. Pam made a right to go home. Lulu and Anna made a left to go back to Main Street.

Anna couldn't wait to get home. She wanted to apologize to Christine. She hoped she'd get some ideas from the face-painting book, too.

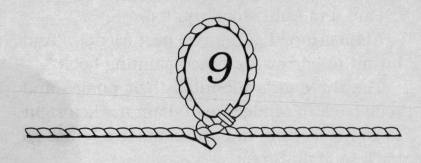

Painting Pals

Anna and Lulu rode into Anna's backyard. Christine was sitting at the picnic table in her aunt's backyard. Her art supplies and a book were on the table.

Christine waved to Anna and Lulu. Anna was glad that Christine was being friendly.

Acorn neighed in Christine's direction. "You'll see Christine later," Anna told him.

"I'll take off Acorn's saddle and cool him down," offered Lulu. "You talk to Christine."

Anna handed Acorn's reins to Lulu and went into Ms. Pucci's backyard.

Anna told Christine that she was sorry for being grumpy and running out of the diner.

Christine apologized for not sharing her face-painting book. "I was afraid my own ideas wouldn't be as good as yours," she said softly.

"I didn't think my ideas would be as good as yours, either," said Anna. "We were both afraid of the same thing."

"I'm sorry," said Christine. "I should have told you about the book before. I was going to at the diner. But you left."

"Can I see it now?" asked Anna.

"Sure," answered Christine. She handed Anna a paperback book titled: *Face Painting*.

Anna flipped through the pages. Christine's cat face, clown face, and flower face were all there.

"I don't like copying them," said Christine. "It's boring. I'd rather make up my own ideas."

"I tried that," said Anna. "It's really hard."

Anna stopped on the page with a lion face. She remembered her own ideas for a lion.

In her mind she pictured a new lion face. It was a combination of her lion face and the book's.

"I have an idea," Anna told Christine. "Can I use your paints?"

"Sure!" agreed Christine.

While Christine watched, Anna quickly drew the outline of a face on paper. Then she painted in a lion face with yellow, white, brown, red, and black paints. When Anna finished, she sat back to look at her lion. Anna thought it looked pretty good.

"Your lion is so great," exclaimed Christine. "It's better than the one in the book!"

"Thanks," said Anna.

Anna flipped through the book again. She stopped on another page.

"Here's their idea for a vampire face," she said. "Let's see if we can make it better. We'll do it together."

Christine drew a face. Anna painted the black parts of the vampire face. Christine did the red parts. She liked painting blood.

When they finished the vampire, they made a rainbow face. They didn't use the book at all for that one.

Lulu came over to the picnic table. She loved the faces that Anna and Christine painted.

"Who did the vampire face?" she asked.

"We both did," said Anna and Christine in unison.

Anna and Christine smiled at each other. It was fun working together.

"We need more paper," Christine told Anna.

"There's a big pad on my desk," said Anna. "It's thick paper."

"We can use it to make the cutout faces for the sign," suggested Christine.

"Good idea," agreed Anna.

"I'll go to Anna's house and get the paper," offered Lulu. "You two keep working. Your ideas are great."

"Can I see the poster again?" asked Anna.

Christine put the poster in the middle of

the table. "It's really good," Anna told her. "Let's fill in the blank faces on the poster together."

"I want to change the cat I copied," said Christine. "It needs more whiskers."

"Some dots on the nose would be cute, too," Anna suggested.

The painting pals filled in the faces on the poster with their new ideas.

"We can bring the poster to my aunt's office and make copies," said Christine.

Anna dipped her brush in red paint. "Lulu can do that," she said, "so we can keep painting."

Christine, Anna, and Lulu worked until dinnertime. By then, they had ten face designs, a pile of posters, and three big faces for the sign.

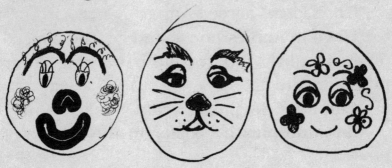

"Tomorrow we can finish the big faces," said Anna. "After your riding lesson."

"And let's practice on each other's faces," suggested Christine. "I'll do your face and you can do mine."

"Perfect," agreed Anna.

"We can do half a face in one design and half in another," giggled Christine.

"Half cat, half flower," joked Anna.

"Half vampire, half rainbow," teased Christine.

Anna felt great. She loved working with another artist. She loved their face-painting ideas.

The next morning, Christine had her second riding lesson. First, Christine, Lulu, and Pam rode around the ring. Then the girls did stretching exercises on their ponies. They reached forward and patted their pony's neck. They reached behind to touch their pony's hip. Next, they did arm circles, one arm at a time.

"Now we'll play games," Mrs. Crandal announced.

Anna threw Christine the ball. Christine caught it easily and tossed it back. The four girls and three ponies played toss-the-ball and serpentine-around-cones. Mrs. Crandal stayed close to Christine. She helped her with posture and balance.

Halfway through the lesson, Anna and Pam traded places. Pam worked on the ground with her mother. Anna rode Lightning.

Anna patted Lightning's neck. "Thanks for letting me ride you, Lightning," she said.

Acorn made a whinny in Anna's direction. He seemed to be saying, "What are you doing on another pony?"

Anna rode Lightning over to Acorn. "You know I love you best," she told her pony. Anna smiled at Christine. "Now we can ride together," she said.

"Thanks again for lending me Acorn," said Christine.

After the lesson Pam and Lulu rode to town. It was time to put up the posters.

Christine and Anna stayed at the Cran-

dals'. They practiced their face designs on the twins and each other.

There were only two more days until the fair. They were very busy days. Christine had two more riding lessons. The Pony Pals and Christine made the big sign for the booth.

Friday was Christine's last night in Wiggins. The four friends had a barbecue supper in the Harleys' backyard.

Anna was in charge of the grill. She cooked hot dogs, burgers, and corn on the cob. Lulu came out with a tray of rolls, salad, catsup, mustard, and relish. Pam was right behind her with a big bottle of soda and cups.

Anna looked around for Christine. She was at the paddock fence with Acorn.

Lulu put the tray down on the picnic table. "Christine's going to miss Acorn," she said.

"Today was her last lesson on him," said Pam. "It was the last time she'll ride him."

"Until she comes back to Wiggins," added Anna.

Anna went back to flipping burgers. Suddenly, she had an idea. She smiled to herself. It would be a wonderful surprise for Christine. Everyone will be surprised, thought Anna.

Walking in the Parade

The next morning, Anna and Lulu groomed their ponies with special care. They wanted them to look their best for the parade.

"No rolling in the dirt today," Anna warned Acorn.

Pam rode off Pony Pal Trail and into the paddock. Lightning's chestnut coat shimmered in the sunlight. Her upside-down heart marking glowed.

Christine came out and admired the three ponies.

"I can't wait to see the Pony Pals riding in the parade," said Christine. "You're going to look so great."

"Our ponies love parades," said Pam. "Especially Acorn."

"Let's finish setting up our booth," suggested Lulu. "The fair officially starts in half an hour."

"My father is putting up the sign for us," Anna told Pam.

Anna and Christine walked together to the town green. Lulu and Pam went to Lulu's house to get the chairs and other supplies.

"I'm excited about the fair," said Christine. "But I feel sad, too."

"Why?" asked Anna.

"I'm going home after the parade," answered Christine. "I had such a good time with the Pony Pals. I'm going to miss you."

Anna put an arm around Christine's shoulder. "We'll miss you, too," Anna said.

The girls reached the face-painting booth.

The sign was up. Mr. Harley was looking at it.

"Nice sign, girls," said Anna's father.

"Thanks, Mr. Harley," said Christine. "And thanks for putting it up."

"We'll paint your face for free, Dad," teased Anna.

"Maybe later," laughed Mr. Harley.

Lulu, Pam, and Lulu's grandmother came out with the chairs, bibs, and mirrors. Dr. Crandal dropped off the two tables. Lulu went back to her house to get the camera and film. Christine checked things off on the TO DO list.

Finally, Christine and the Pony Pals were ready for business.

Jack and Jill were their first customers. Next, Rosalie and Mike Lacey came to the booth.

"Sorry I bugged you the other day on Lilac Lane," Mike told Anna.

"You didn't bother me," she said. "Just forget it, okay?"

"Okay," agreed Mike.

"Will you do me a favor with your bike?" asked Anna.

"I guess," he said. "What is it?"

Anna whispered to Mike what the favor was. He agreed to do it.

"It's a surprise," she concluded. "Don't tell anyone."

Out of the corner of her eye, Anna saw Tommy Rand. He was walking toward the face-painting booth. Mike saw him, too.

"Mike, can you keep Tommy away from our booth?" Anna asked. "He'll only cause trouble."

"Okay," agreed Mike.

Mike ran over to Tommy. The two boys disappeared into the crowd.

I hope Mike doesn't forget to go to Pam's for me, thought Anna. If he forgets, it will ruin my surprise.

The face-painting booth was very popular. Pam collected money and kept the line orderly. Anna and Christine painted rainbows, flowers, vampires, cats, and lions. Lulu took photographs.

Christine and Anna took turns taking a lunch break. There was always someone to paint faces and collect money.

During Anna's break, she ran over to the paddock and looked in the pony shed. Mike had done what she asked. The special riding girth was there.

Christine had lunch with her parents. After lunch, she brought them to the face-painting booth. Christine introduced her parents to the Pony Pals.

Christine's mother thanked them for helping Christine ride. "It's been the best physical therapy for Christine," said Mrs. Pucci.

"She's standing taller and her balance is better."

"And I had a good time," added Christine. "I love riding." She smiled at the Pony Pals. "I'm going to take lessons when I go home."

Christine sat down at her face-painting table. A sweet-looking girl sat in front of her. "I want to be a vampire," she said.

"I have to go back to work," Christine told her parents.

"We're leaving at five," Christine's mother reminded her. "It's a long ride home."

"Okay," agreed Christine. "As long as we see the Pony Pals in the parade."

"We wouldn't miss the parade," said Christine's mother. "I'm looking forward to seeing the Pony Pals ride."

"Especially you and Acorn, Anna," Christine's father added. "We've heard all about your pony."

"Watch Acorn," Anna told him. "Acorn's full of surprises."

Mr. and Mrs. Pucci went off to see the other booths at the fair.

Christine painted pointy black eyebrows on the little girl.

Anna painted half-circles of rainbow colors on a boy's face. She started with a small purple curve on his nose and ended with a wide red stripe going from cheek to cheek across his forehead.

"Now you are a perfect rainbow," Anna told the little boy. She held up the hand mirror so he could see himself.

"Wow!" exclaimed the boy. "I'm never going to wash my face again."

At three-thirty, the face-painting booth closed for business. It was time to saddle up the ponies for the parade.

"I'll watch you from my aunt's front porch," Christine told them.

"Come to the paddock while we get ready," suggested Anna. "Acorn will want to see you."

When the four girls reached the paddock, Anna told them she had a surprise.

"What?" the three girls asked in unison.

"Christine is going to ride Acorn in the parade," she said.

"But you're supposed to ride Acorn," said Christine. "He's your pony."

"I ride Acorn in plenty of parades," Anna told her. "This time I'll walk. I'll lead you and Acorn."

"Are you sure you don't want to ride, Anna?" asked Lulu.

"I want Christine to ride in this parade," said Anna. She smiled at Christine. "Your parents will see you. It'll be great."

"They'll be so surprised," exclaimed Christine.

"There's one big problem," said Pam. "The saddle is too big for Christine. The riding girth is in my barn." She looked at her watch. "There isn't enough time to get it."

"I thought of that," said Anna. "Mike picked it up for us. I asked him this morning." She grinned at her friends. "The girth is in the shed. Christine can ride."

"You thought of everything, Anna," said Christine. "Thank you."

When the four girls had reached the paddock, Acorn trotted over to greet them.

"I'm going to ride you in the parade," Christine told him.

Acorn nodded as if he understood.

A few minutes later the three riders were on their ponies.

Anna led Christine and Acorn to the head of the parade line. Lulu followed on Snow White. Pam and Lightning were behind them.

The band was getting ready behind the ponies. The fire trucks were lined up behind the band. A trumpet sounded the signal for the opening of the parade.

Anna turned to Christine. "Ready?" she asked.

"Ready," she answered. She beamed a big smile.

Anna loved leading Acorn and Christine in the parade. Acorn walked with his head held high and a smart, proud step. When they

passed the Pucci house, Christine's parents and aunt waved and cheered. Christine waved back to them. Anna waved, too.

After Christine went home, Anna and Lulu led their ponies to the paddock. They took off their tacks, wiped them down, and gave them hay and food.

Anna sat on a hay bale and watched the ponies. When Acorn finished eating he walked over to her. He bowed. She hadn't given him the signal to bow. Next, Acorn dropped his head onto Anna's lap.

Tears of happiness sprang to her eyes.

Anna stroked Acorn's cheek. You are the most wonderful pony in the world, she thought. And you really are mine.